U0025449

Tales from Shakespeare

A Midsummer
Night's Dream
&
As You Like It

悅讀莎士比亞故事 (3)

仲。夏。夜。之。夢

皆。大。歡。喜

Charles and Mary Lamb

CONTENTS

CONTENTS

附本

威廉‧莎士比亞（William Shakespeare, 1564-1616）

Shakespeare Centre, Henley St. Stratford-upon-Avon, Warwickshire

莎士比亞簡介

陳敬旻

威廉・莎士比亞（William Shakespeare）出生於英國的史特拉福（Stratford-upon-Avon）。莎士比亞的父親曾任地方議員，母親是地主的女兒。莎士比亞對婦女在廚房或起居室裡勞動的描繪不少，這大概是經由觀察母親所得。他本人也懂得園藝，故作品中的植草種樹表現鮮活。

1571 年，莎士比亞進入公立學校就讀，校內教學多採拉丁文，因此在其作品中到處可見到羅馬詩人奧維德（Ovid）的影子。當時代古典文學的英譯日漸普遍，有學者認為莎士比亞只懂得英語，但這種說法有可議之處。舉例來說，在高登的譯本裡，森林女神只用 Diana 這個名字，而莎士比亞卻在《仲夏夜之夢》一劇中用奧維德原作中的 Titania 一名來稱呼仙后。和莎士比亞有私交的文學家班・強生（Ben Jonson）則曾說，莎翁「懂得一點拉丁文，和一點點希臘文」。

莎士比亞的劇本亦常引用聖經典故，顯示他對新舊約也頗為熟悉。在伊麗莎白女王時期，通俗英語中已有很多聖經詞語。此外，莎士比亞應該很知悉當時代年輕人所流行的遊戲娛樂，當時也應該有巡迴劇團不時前來史特拉福演出。 1575 年，伊麗莎白女王來到郡上時，當地人以化裝遊行、假面戲劇、煙火來款待女王，《仲夏夜之夢》裡就有這種盛會的描繪。

1582 年，莎士比亞與安·海瑟威（Anne Hathaway）結婚，但這場婚姻顯得草率，連莎士比亞的雙親都因不知情而沒有出席婚禮。 1586 年，他們在倫敦定居下來。 1586 年的倫敦已是英國首都，年輕人莫不想在此大展抱負。史特拉福與倫敦之間的交通頻仍，但對身無長物的人而言，步行仍是最平常的旅行方式。伊麗莎白時期的文學家喜好步行， 1618 年，班·強生就曾在倫敦與愛丁堡之間徒步來回。

莎士比亞初抵倫敦的史料不充足，引發諸多揣測。其中一說為莎士比亞曾在律師處當職員，因為他在劇本與詩歌中經常提及法律術語。但這種說法站不住腳，因為莎士比亞多有訛用，例如他在《威尼斯商人》和《一報還一報》中提到的法律原理及程序，就有諸多錯誤。

事實上，伊麗莎白時期的作家都喜歡引用法律詞彙，這是因為當時的文人和律師時有往來，而且中產階級也常介入訴訟案件，許多法律術語自然為常人所知。莎士比亞樂於援用法律術語，這顯示了他對當代生活和風尚的興趣。莎士比亞自抵達倫敦到告老還鄉，心思始終放在戲劇和詩歌上，不太可能接受法律這門專業領域的訓練。

莎士比亞在倫敦的第一份工作是劇場工作。當時常態營業的劇場有兩個：「劇場」（the Theatre）和「帷幕」（the Curtain）。「劇場」的所有人為詹姆士·波比奇（James Burbage），莎士比亞就在此落腳。「劇場」財務狀況不佳，1596 年波比奇過世，把「劇場」交給兩個兒子，其中一個兒子便是著名的悲劇演員理查·波比奇（Richard Burbage）。後來「劇場」因租約問題無法解決，決定將原有的建築物拆除，在泰晤士河的對面重建，改名為「環球」（the Globe）。不久，「環球」就展開了戲劇史上空前繁榮的時代。

伊麗莎白時期的戲劇表演只有男演員，所有的女性角色都由男性擔任。演員反串時會戴上面具，效果十足，然而這並不損故事的意境。莎士比亞本身也是一位出色的演員，曾在《皆大歡喜》和《哈姆雷特》中分別扮演忠僕亞當和國王鬼魂這兩個角色。

莎士比亞很留意演員的説白道詞，這點可從哈姆雷特告誡伶人的對話中窺知一二。莎士比亞熟稔劇場的技術與運作，加上他也是劇場股東，故對劇場的營運和組織都甚有研究。不過，他的志業不在演出或劇場管理，而是劇本和詩歌創作。

莎士比亞的戲劇創作始於 1591 年，他當時真正師法的對象是擅長喜劇的約翰・李利（John Lyly），以及曾寫下轟動一時的悲劇《帖木兒大帝》（Tamburlaine the Great）的克里斯多夫・馬婁（Christopher Marlowe）。莎翁戲劇的特色是兼容並蓄，吸收各家長處，而且他也勤奮多產。一直到 1611 年封筆之前，他每年平均寫出兩部劇作和三卷詩作。莎士比亞慣於在既有的文學作品中尋找材料，又重視大眾喜好，常能讓平淡無奇的作品廣受喜愛。

在當時，劇本都是賣斷給劇場，不能再賣給出版商，因此莎劇的出版先後，並不能反映其創作的時間先後。莎翁作品的先後順序都由後人所推斷，推測的主要依據是作品題材和韻格。他早期的戲劇作品，無論悲劇或喜劇，性質都很單純。隨著創作的手法逐漸成熟，內容愈來愈複雜深刻，悲喜劇熔冶一爐。

自 1591 年席德尼爵士（Sir Philip Sidney）的十四行詩集發表後，十四行詩（sonnets，另譯為商籟）在英國即普遍受到文人的喜愛與仿傚。其中許多作品承續佩脫拉克（Petrarch）的風格，多描寫愛情的酸甜苦樂。莎士比亞的創作一向很能反應當時代的文學風尚，在詩歌體裁鼎盛之時，他也將才華展現在十四行詩上，並將部分作品寫入劇本之中。

莎士比亞的十四行詩主要有兩個主題：婚姻責任和詩歌的不朽。這兩者皆是文藝復興時期詩歌中常見的主題。不少人以為莎士比亞的十四行詩表達了他個人的自省與懺悔，但事實上這些內容有更多是源於他的戲劇天分。

1595 年至 1598 年，莎士比亞陸續寫了《羅密歐與茱麗葉》、《仲夏夜之夢》、《馴悍記》、《威尼斯商人》和若干歷史劇，他的詩歌戲劇也在這段時期受到肯定。當時代的梅爾斯（Francis Meres）就將莎士比亞視為最偉大的文學家，他說：「要是繆思會說英語，一定也會喜歡引用莎士比亞的精彩語藻。」「無論是悲劇或喜劇，莎士比亞的表現都是首屈一指。」

闊別故鄉十一年後，莎士比亞於 1596 年返回故居，並在隔年買下名為「新居」（New Place）的房子。那是鎮上第二大的房子，他大幅改建整修，爾後家道日益興盛。莎士比亞有足夠的財力置產並不足以為奇，但他大筆的固定收入主要來自表演，而非劇本創作。當時不乏有成功的演員靠演戲發財，甚至有人將這種現象寫成劇本。

除了表演之外，劇場行政及管理的工作，還有宮廷演出的賞賜，都是他的財源。許多文獻均顯示，莎士比亞是個非常關心財富、地產和社會地位的人，讓許多人感到與他的詩人形象有些扞格不入。

伊麗莎白女王過世後，詹姆士一世（James I）於 1603 年登基，他把莎士比亞所屬的劇團納入保護。莎士比亞此時寫了《第十二夜》和佳評如潮的《哈姆雷特》，成就傲視全英格蘭。但他仍謙恭有禮、溫文爾雅，一如十多前年初抵倫敦的樣子，因此也愈發受到大眾的喜愛。

從這一年起，莎士比亞開始撰寫悲劇《奧賽羅》。他寫悲劇並非是因為精神壓力或生活變故，而是身為一名劇作家，最終目的就是要寫出優秀的悲劇作品。當時他嘗試以詩入劇，在《哈姆雷特》和《一報還一報》中尤其爐火純青。隨後《李爾王》和《馬克白》問世，一直到四年後的《安東尼與克麗奧佩脫拉》，寫作風格登峰造極。

1609 年，倫敦瘟疫猖獗，隔年不見好轉，46 歲的莎士比亞決定告別倫敦，返回史特拉福退隱。 1616 年，莎士比亞和老友德雷頓、班·強生聚會時，可能由於喝得過於盡興，回家後發高燒，一病不起。他將遺囑修改完畢，同年 4 月 23 日，恰巧在他 52 歲的生日當天去世。

七年後，昔日的劇團好友收錄他的劇本做為全集出版，其中有喜劇、歷史劇、悲劇等共 36 個劇本。此書不僅不負莎翁本人所託，也為後人留下珍貴而豐富的文化資源，其中不僅包括美妙動人的詞句，還有各種人物的性格塑造，如高貴、低微、嚴肅或歡樂等性格的著墨。

除了作品，莎士比亞本人也在生前受到讚揚。班・強生曾說他是個「正人君子，天性開放自由，想像力出奇，擁有大無畏的思想，言詞溫和，蘊含機智。」也有學者以勇敢、敏感、平衡、幽默和身心健康這五種特質來形容莎士比亞，並說他「將無私的愛奉為至上，認為罪惡的根源是恐懼，而非金錢。」

值得一提的是，有人認為這些劇本刻畫入微，具有知性，不可能是未受過大學教育的莎士比亞所寫，因而引發爭議。有人就此推測真正的作者，其中較為人知的有法蘭西斯・培根（Francis Bacon）和牛津的德維爾公爵（Edward de Vere of Oxford），後者形成了頗具影響力的牛津學派。儘管傳說繪聲繪影，各種假說和研究不斷，但大概已經沒有人會懷疑確有莎士比亞這個人的存在了。

作者簡介：蘭姆姐弟

陳敬旻

姐姐瑪麗（Mary Lamb）生於 1764 年，弟弟查爾斯（Charles Lamb）於 1775 年也在倫敦呱呱落地。因為家境不夠寬裕，瑪麗沒有接受過完整的教育。她從小就做針線活，幫忙持家，照顧母親。查爾斯在學生時代結識了詩人柯立芝（Samuel Taylor Coleridge），兩人成為終生的朋友。查爾斯後來因家中經濟困難而輟學， 1792 年轉而就職於東印度公司（East India House），這是他謀生的終身職業。

查爾斯在二十歲時一度精神崩潰，瑪麗則因為長年工作過量，在 1796 年突然精神病發，持刀攻擊父母，母親不幸傷重身亡。這件人倫悲劇發生後，瑪麗被判為精神異常，送往精神病院。查爾斯為此放棄自己原本期待的婚姻，以便全心照顧姐姐，使她免於在精神病院終老。

十九世紀的英國教育重視莎翁作品，一般的中產階級家庭也希望孩子早點接觸莎劇。1806 年，文學家兼編輯高德溫（William Godwin）邀請查爾斯協助「少年圖書館」的出版計畫，請他將莎翁的劇本改寫為適合兒童閱讀的故事。

查爾斯接受這項工作後就與瑪麗合作，他負責六齣悲劇，瑪麗負責十四齣喜劇並撰寫前言。瑪麗在後來曾描述説，他們兩人「就坐在同一張桌子上改寫，看起來就好像《仲夏夜之夢》裡的荷米雅與海蓮娜一樣。」就這樣，姐弟兩人合力完成了這一系列的莎士比亞故事。《莎士比亞故事集》在 1807 年出版後便大受好評，建立了查爾斯的文學聲譽。

查爾斯的寫作風格獨特，筆法樸實，主題豐富。他將自己的一生，包括童年時代、基督教會學校的生活、東印度公司的光陰、與瑪麗相伴的點點滴滴，以及自己的白日夢、鍾愛的書籍和友人等等，都融入在文章裡，作品充滿細膩情感和豐富的想像力。他的軟弱、怪異、魅力、幽默、口吃，在在都使讀者感到親切熟悉，而獨特的筆法與敘事方式，也使他成為英國出色的散文大師。

1823 年，查爾斯和瑪麗領養了一個孤兒愛瑪。兩年後，查爾斯自東印度公司退休，獲得豐厚的退休金。查爾斯的健康情形和瑪麗的精神狀況卻每況愈下。 1833 年，愛瑪嫁給出版商後，又只剩下姐弟兩人。 1834 年 7 月，由於幼年時代的好友柯立芝去世，查爾斯的精神一蹶不振，沉湎酒精。此年秋天，查爾斯在散步時不慎跌倒，傷及顏面，後來傷口竟惡化至不可收拾的地步，而於年底過世。

查爾斯善與人交，他和同時期的許多文人都保持良好情誼，又因他一生對姐姐的照顧不餘遺力，所以也廣受敬佩。查爾斯和瑪麗兩人都終生未婚，查爾斯曾在一篇伊利亞小品中，將他們的狀況形容為「雙重單身」（double singleness）。查爾斯去世後，瑪麗的心理狀態雖然漸趨惡化，但仍繼續活了十三年之久。

A Midsummer Night's Dream

仲夏夜之夢

導讀

陳敬旻

《仲夏夜之夢》是莎劇中最常被搬演改編也是最受歡迎的喜劇之一，有不少人都還是透過《仲夏夜之夢》開始接觸到莎翁作品。近幾十年來，此劇因為含有夢的成分，因此受到不少心理分析大師的青睞。又因內容提及父親意圖掌握女兒、仙王意欲控制仙后的橋段，因此也有人引用女性主義來探討此劇。

本劇敘述雅典城內的一對戀人荷米雅和萊桑德，荷米雅的父親反對他們在一起，他要求公爵下令，若荷米雅不肯嫁給德米崔斯，就要判她死罪。於是荷米雅和萊桑德決定逃出雅典，而喜歡荷米雅的德米崔斯，以及迷戀德米崔斯的海蓮娜，亦跟隨這對戀人逃進森林。

林子裡的仙王歐伯龍為幫助海蓮娜，就命令帕克趁德米崔斯睡著時，把神奇的情水滴在他的眼皮上，待他醒來，就會愛上睜眼後第一個看到的人。未料陰錯陽差，帕克搞錯對象，把情水滴在萊桑德的眼上，使萊桑德愛上海蓮娜。

歐伯龍得知後，趕緊把情水滴在德米崔斯的眼睛裡，讓他也愛上海蓮娜，然後再把解藥倒進萊桑德的眼睛裡解除魔法。荷米雅的父親發現荷米雅和德米崔斯各有意中人後，也就答應了兩人的婚事。最後，這兩對戀人就雙雙在同一天舉行婚禮。

真實與夢幻

整場戲就情節推演而言，可分三個部分：首先是一條地位崇高卻荒謬無比的律法；其次，劇中男女人物逃往林子後，精靈的介入使彼此愛的對象混淆，因而產生誤解與衝突；最後，一陣混亂之後，終於恢復理智和諧。本故事發生在仲夏夜晚，故事的主人翁們一度失去自我，事實上在西方文化中，有所謂的「仲夏瘋」（midsummer madness）和「月暈」（moonstruck），便象徵著黎明之時，混亂才能回復秩序，疑惑衝突才會得到解決。

此劇兩兩對比的元素，如幾何圖形般對稱，故事發生於城市與森林、清醒與睡眠、真實與夢幻之間。底修斯掌管現實的雅典城，歐伯龍則是夢幻的森林之王，分別象徵理智和潛意識。

森林代表激情、焦慮、混亂、不受管束，隱藏著許多不可預測的因素，甚至有身分錯置的危機，彷彿是一場紛擾的夢境，時空與真實世界截然不同。雅典城代表社會機制和社會運作的秩序，足以化解所有的衝突。

鄉巴佬和帕克這兩個角色，恰可以做為真實世界與夢幻世界的代表人物。庸俗也好，質樸也罷，許多評論家特別中意鄉巴佬這個角色，認為他腳踏實地，對仙后的地位和法力不為所動，只關心找到路回家、覓食、搔癢、睡覺。帕克則是抱持遊戲人間的態度，他捉弄村民，對自己找錯對象、滴錯情水不但不以為意，還覺得很有趣味，代表了對脫序狀態的偏好。

另一個對稱的安排是兩兩成雙的戀人，萊桑德和德米崔斯，荷米雅和海蓮娜，他們之間的角色互換，撲朔迷離。

原創性的劇情

本劇看似簡單，實則具有不凡的文學與戲劇價值。另外，在莎翁眾多的劇本當中，《仲夏夜之夢》也是少數極具原創性的劇本，不像其大部分的劇本，取材其他作品而融合改編。

此劇約於 1595-1596 年間完成，雖然可能只是為一般大眾而寫的通俗劇，但也有部分學者認為是因應某節慶或某貴族婚禮而寫就演出，所以充滿希望和歡娛氣氛。現代曆法的仲夏指的是六月二十四日，但劇中提及五月節慶，所以故事發生的時間可能在五月。在早期，只有夏秋冬三個季節，夏天包含春天，所以仲夏便落在五月初，但莎士比亞並沒有明白點出確切的時間背景。

莎士比亞在當時期似乎特別偏好「夢」，在同時期的作品《理查二世》和《羅密歐與茱麗葉》中，「夢」字的出現也特別頻繁，其在這三個劇本中出現的次數，就佔了他所有劇作的三分之一。夢境光怪陸離，醒來之後，雖知其不可思議，卻不會令人無法接受，這就是夢的特質。潛意識藉由我們可感知的方式，在夢裡呈現出來。夢處理不同於理性的情緒，透露我們的真正想法、感覺、欲望或恐懼等等，揭露隱而不見的潛意識。夢也帶有預示作用，預示未來的可能變化。

據此，仲夏夜之「夢」屬於預示的夢，夢醒後，戀情圓滿成雙，好友重修舊好，死罪撤銷。但仲夏夜之「夢」又不是真正的夢，夢醒後之所以圓滿，乃是因為精靈從中介入。所以劇終時，劇中人才會告訴觀眾讀者，如果本劇顯得似是而非、不合情理，那就當看戲是做夢，就把整齣戲看作是一場夢吧。

精靈與魔法

提到精靈，伊莉莎白時期的人們大都相信精靈的存在，鄉間尤其流傳精靈傳說。他們認為精靈和祖先凱爾特人（Celtic）同源，會騎馬打獵、跳舞歡宴，也能夠變身或是飛天隱形。精靈既對凡人慷慨贈與，也會懲戒凡人。他們處罰人類的方式常常是捏擰一把，或是用醜小孩來和人類的小孩調包。這些精靈一般都稱為帕克（puck，意指淘氣、喜歡惡作劇的小妖精）或者小妖魔（hobgoblin），他們多半喜歡在夜晚作怪，有些邪惡意味，有些大人會拿這些小妖怪來嚇唬不聽話的孩子。

此外，神話傳說中的仙王一般就叫做歐伯龍（Oberon），仙后則稱為戴安娜（Diana）、辛西亞（Cynthia）、妃比（Phoebe）或黑克悌（Hecate）等，而仙王的地位通常略遜於仙后。漸漸地，人們不再信仰精靈，但精靈仍成為通俗的娛樂文化中受人歡迎的主題，尤其是台上歌舞表演的主要角色。《仲夏夜之夢》中對仙王、仙后和帕克的描述，大致與傳說吻合，這顯示莎士比亞熟悉民間傳說。他直接沿用各種傳說，唯獨仙后泰坦妮的名字取自歐維德的《變形記》。另外，帕克愛捉弄人，卻無惡意，這似乎也是莎翁的創舉。

本齣戲中的有許多場景特別適於劇場表現，例如夏夜森林、森林精靈、精靈魔法、好事多磨的兩對戀人，或是仙后和驢頭鄉巴佬的滑稽邂逅等等。事實上，這部戲的演出史可以說就是精靈的造型史。十九世紀起，精靈的演出常由數十位歌者或舞者集體表現，他們或為兒童，或為少年，或為成人。此時，甚至也出現了東方造型的精靈。

此劇歷久不衰，深受喜愛。其一般的製作和演出，傾向以芭蕾劇或歌劇呈現，其中最著名的舞台演出是英國導演彼得・布魯克（Peter Brook）於 1970 年的作品，近年來則有羅伯・樂帕許（Robert Lepage）為英國國家劇院（National Theatre）執導的版本，有興趣的讀者可參考葛瑞飛茲（Trevor R. Griffiths）所編纂的《仲夏夜之夢》演出紀錄，而喜好電影的讀者，也可能看過多部電影版的《仲夏夜之夢》。

人物表

Oberon	歐伯龍	精靈國的仙王
Titania	泰坦妮	精靈國的仙后
Puck	帕克	精靈，歐伯龍的差使
Hermia	荷米雅	因父親將她許配給德米崔斯，準備和情人萊桑德私奔
Lysander	萊桑德	和荷米雅是一對戀人
Helena	海蓮娜	荷米雅的好友，喜歡德米崔斯
Demetrius	德米崔斯	一位貴族青年

A Midsummer
Night's Dream

Hermia and Helena

There was a law in the city of Athens which gave to its citizens the power of compelling[1] their daughters to marry whomsoever they pleased; for upon a daughter's refusing to marry the man her father had chosen to be her husband, the father was empowered by this law to cause her to be put to death; but as fathers do not often desire the death of their own daughters, even though they do happen to prove a little refractory[2], this law was seldom or never put in execution[3], though perhaps the young ladies of that city were not unfrequently threatened by their parents with the terrors of it.

There was one instance, however, of an old man, whose name was Egeus, who actually did come before Theseus (at that time the reigning duke of Athens), to complain that his daughter Hermia, whom he had commanded to marry Demetrius, a young man of a noble Athenian family, refused to obey him, because she loved another young Athenian, named Lysander. Egeus demanded justice of Theseus, and desired that this cruel law might be put in force against his daughter.

1 compel [kəm'pel] (v.) 強迫
2 refractory [rɪ'fræktəri] (a.) 執拗的
3 execution [ˌeksɪ'kjuːʃən] (n.) 執行；實行

2 Hermia pleaded[4] in excuse for her disobedience, that Demetrius had formerly professed love for her dear friend Helena, and that Helena loved Demetrius to distraction[5]; but this honorable reason, which Hermia gave for not obeying her father's command, moved not the stern Egeus.

Hermia and Helena

Theseus, though a great and merciful prince, had no power to alter the laws of his country; therefore he could only give Hermia four days to consider of it and at the end of that time, if she still refused to marry Demetrius, she was to be put to death.

When Hermia was dismissed from the presence of the duke, she went to her lover Lysander, and told him the peril[6] she was in, and that she must either give him up and marry Demetrius, or lose her life in four days.

---

4 plead [pliːd] (v.) 抗辯
5 distraction [dɪˈstrækʃən] (n.) 發狂
6 peril [ˈperəl] (n.) 危險

Lysander was in great affliction[7] at hearing these evil tidings[8]; but recollecting that he had an aunt who lived at some distance from Athens, and that at the place where she lived the cruel law could not be put in force against Hermia (this law not extending beyond the boundaries of the city), he proposed to Hermia that she should steal out of her father's house that night, and go with him to his aunt's house, where he would marry her.

"I will meet you," said Lysander, "in the wood a few miles without the city; in that delightful wood where we have so often walked with Helena in the pleasant month of May."

---

7 affliction [əˈflɪkʃən] (n.) 痛苦；苦難
8 tidings [ˈtaɪdɪŋz] (n.)〔古代用法〕（複數形）消息；音信

To this proposal Hermia joyfully agreed; and she told no one of her intended flight[9] but her friend Helena. Helena (as maidens will do foolish things for love) very ungenerously resolved[10] to go and tell this to Demetrius, though she could hope no benefit from betraying her friend's secret, but the poor pleasure of following her faithless lover to the wood; for she well knew that Demetrius would go thither[11] in pursuit of Hermia.

Hermia told no one of her intended flight but her friend Helena.

The wood in which Lysander and Hermia proposed to meet, was the favorite haunt of those little beings known by the name of *Fairies*.

9 flight [flaɪt] (n.) 逃亡；逃走
10 resolve [rɪˈzɑːlv] (v.) 決定；決心
11 thither [ˈθɪðər] (adv.) 〔舊時用法〕到彼處

🎧 5   Oberon the king, and Titania the queen of the Fairies, with all their tiny train[12] of followers, in this wood held their midnight revels[13].

    Between this little king and queen of sprites there happened, at this time, a sad disagreement; they never met by moonlight in the shady walks of this pleasant wood, but they were quarreling, till all their fairy elves[14] would creep[15] into acorn-cups and hide themselves for fear.

12 train [treɪn] (n.) 成縱隊行進的若干人、車輛等隊伍
13 revel ['revəl] (n.) 作樂；狂歡享樂
14 elf [elf] (n.) 小精靈（複數形作 elves）
15 creep [kriːp] (v.) 爬行；匍匐

PUCK   And now they never meet in grove or green,
       By fountain clear, or spangled starlight sheen,
       But, they do square.

                                         Act 2. Scene 1.

🎧 The cause of this unhappy disagreement was Titania's refusing to give Oberon a little changeling[16] boy, whose mother had been Titania's friend; and upon her death the fairy queen stole the child from its nurse, and brought him up in the woods.

The night on which the lovers were to meet in this wood, as Titania was walking with some of her maids of honor, she met Oberon attended by his train of fairy courtiers[17].

"Ill met by moonlight, proud Titania," said the fairy king.

The queen replied, "What, jealous Oberon, is it you? Fairies, skip hence; I have forsworn[18] his company."

"Tarry[19], rash fairy," said Oberon; "am not I thy lord? Why does Titania cross her Oberon? Give me your little changeling boy to be my page[20]."

"Set your heart at rest," answered the queen; "your whole fairy kingdom buys not the boy of me." She then left her lord in great anger.

"Well, go your way," said Oberon: "before the morning dawns I will torment[21] you for this injury."

---

16 changeling ['tʃeɪndʒlɪŋ] (n.) 調包小孩（傳說仙神調包後的小孩）
17 courtier ['kɔːrtɪr] (n.) 朝臣
18 forswear [fɔr'swɛr] (v.) 放棄；戒絕
19 tarry ['tæri] (v.) 逗留；停留
20 page [peɪdʒ] (n.) 僮僕
21 torment ['tɔːrment] (v.) 折磨

The Quarrel of Oberon and Titania

Oberon and Puck

7 Oberon then sent for Puck, his chief favorite and privy counselor.

Puck (or as he was sometimes called, Robin Goodfellow) was a shrewd[22] and knavish[23] sprite, that used to play comical pranks in the neighboring villages; sometimes getting into the dairies and skimming the milk, sometimes plunging[24] his light and airy form into the butter-churn[25], and while he was dancing his fantastic shape in the churn, in vain the dairy-maid would labor to change her cream into butter: nor had the village swains[26] any better success; whenever Puck chose to play his freaks[27] in the brewing copper[28], the ale was sure to be spoiled.

---

22 shrewd [ʃruːd] (a.) 狡獪的
23 knavish [ˈneɪvɪʃ] (a.) 無賴的
24 plunge [plʌndʒ] (v.) 投入
25 butter-churn [ˈbʌtər͵tʃɜːrn] (n.) 攪乳器
26 swain [sweɪn] (n.) 〔詩的用法〕〔古代用法〕年輕的鄉下人
27 freak [friːk] (n.) 怪誕的思想、行動或事件
28 copper [ˈkɑːpər] (n.) 金屬鍋

8 When a few good neighbors were met to drink some comfortable ale together, Puck would jump into the bowl of ale in the likeness of a roasted crab, and when some old goody[29] was going to drink he would bob[30] against her lips, and spill the ale over her withered chin; and presently

"— down topples she."

after, when the same old dame was gravely seating herself to tell her neighbors a sad and melancholy story, Puck would slip her three-legged stool from under her, and down toppled[31] the poor old woman, and then the old gossips would hold their sides[32] and laugh at her, and swear they never wasted a merrier hour.

29 goody [ˈgʊdi] (n.) 低下階層的老婦
30 bob [bɑːb] (v.) 上下移動
31 topple [ˈtɑːpəl] (v.) 搖搖欲墜
32 hold their sides 捧腹大笑

🎧⁹ "Come hither, Puck," said Oberon to this little merry wanderer of the night; "fetch me the flower which maids call Love in Idleness; the juice of that little purple flower laid on the eyelids of those who sleep, will make them, when they awake, dote[33] on the first thing they see. Some of the juice of that flower I will drop on the eyelids of my Titania when she is asleep; and the first thing she looks upon when she opens her eyes she will fall in love with, even though it be a lion or a bear, a meddling[34] monkey, or a busy ape; and before I will take this charm from off her sight, which I can do with another charm I know of, I will make her give me that boy to be my page."

Oberon

33 dote [doʊt] (v.) 溺愛；寵
34 meddling ['medlɪŋ] (a.) 妨礙的；干擾的

Puck, who loved mischief to his heart, was highly diverted with this intended frolic[35] of his master, and ran to seek the flower; and while Oberon was waiting the return of Puck, he observed Demetrius and Helena enter the wood: he overheard Demetrius reproaching Helena for following him, and after many unkind words on his part, and gentle expostulations[36] from Helena, reminding him of his former love and professions of true faith to her, he left her (as he said) to the mercy of the wild beasts, and she ran after him as swiftly as she could.

---

35 frolic ['frɑːlɪk] (n.) 嬉戲；作樂
36 expostulation [ɪkˌspɑːstʃuˈleɪʃən] (n.) 告誡；勸誡

The fairy king, who was always friendly to true lovers, felt great compassion for Helena; and perhaps, as Lysander said they used to walk by moonlight in this pleasant wood, Oberon might have seen Helena in those happy times when she was beloved by Demetrius.

However that might be, when Puck returned with the little purple flower, Oberon said to his favorite, "Take a part of this flower; there has been a sweet Athenian lady here, who is in love with a disdainful[37] youth; if you find him sleeping, drop some of the love-juice in his eyes, but contrive[38] to do it when she is near him, that the first thing he sees when he awakes may be this despised[39] lady. You will know the man by the Athenian garments which he wears."

37 disdainful [dɪsˈdeɪnfəl] (a.) 輕蔑的
38 contrive [kənˈtraɪv] (v.) 想辦法；動腦筋
39 despised [dɪˈspaɪzd] (a.) 受人輕視的

(12) Puck promised to manage this matter very dexterously[40]: and then Oberon went, unperceived by Titania, to her bower[41], where she was preparing to go to rest. Her fairy bower was a bank, where grew wild thyme[42], cowslips, and sweet violets, under a canopy[43] of woodbine, musk-roses, and eglantine[44]. There Titania always slept some part of the night; her coverlet the enameled[45] skin of a snake, which, though a small mantle[46], was wide enough to wrap a fairy in.

He found Titania giving orders to her fairies, how they were to employ themselves while she slept. "Some of you," said her majesty, "must kill cankers[47] in the musk-rose buds, and some wage war with the bats for their leathern wings, to make my small elves coats; and some of you keep watch that the clamorous[48] owl, that nightly hoots[49], come not near me: but first sing me to sleep."

Then they began to sing this song—

---

40 dexterously [ˈdekstərəsli] (adv.) 雙手靈巧地
41 bower [ˈbauər] (n.) 〔文學用法〕閨房
42 thyme [taɪm] (n.) 百里香
43 canopy [ˈkænəpi] (n.) 野櫻草
44 eglantine [ˈegləntaɪn] (n.) 野薔薇
45 enameled [ɪˈnæməld] (a.) 瓷釉的
46 mantle [ˈmæntl] (n.) 斗篷；〔比喻用法〕覆蓋物
47 canker [ˈkæŋkər] (n.) 動、植物的潰瘍病
48 clamorous [ˈklæmərəs] (a.) 吵鬧的；叫喊的
49 hoot [huːt] (n.) 梟叫聲

NEWTS, AND BLIND-WORMS, DO NO WRONG;
COME NOT NEAR OUR FAIRY QUEEN:

You spotted snakes with double tongue,
Thorny hedgehogs[50], be not seen;
Newts[51] and blindworms, do no wrong,
Come not near our Fairy Queen.
Philomel[52], with melody,
Sing in our sweet lullaby,
Lulla, lulla, lullaby; lulla, lulla, lullaby;
Never harm, nor spell, nor charm,
Come our lovely lady nigh[53];
So good night with lullaby.

50 hedgehog [ˈhedʒhɑːg] (n.) 刺蝟
51 newt [njuːt] (n.) 蠑螈
52 philomel [ˈfɪləmel] (n.) 夜鶯
53 nigh [naɪ] (adv.) (prep.) 〔古代用法〕〔詩的用法〕靠近

When the fairies had sung their queen asleep with this pretty lullaby, they left her to perform the important services she had enjoined them. Oberon then softly drew near his Titania, and dropped some of the love-juice on her eyelids, saying—

What thou seest when them dost[54] wake,
Do it for thy true-love take.

---

54 dost [dʌst] (v.)〔古代用法〕do 的第二人稱單數，與 thou 連用

But to return to Hermia, who made her escape out of her father's house that night, to avoid the death she was doomed to for refusing to marry Demetrius. When she entered the wood, she found her dear Lysander waiting for her, to conduct her to his aunt's house; but before they had passed half through the wood, Hermia was so much fatigued, that Lysander, who was very careful of this dear lady, who had proved her affection for him even by hazarding[55] her life for his sake, persuaded her to rest till morning on a bank of soft moss, and lying down himself on the ground at some little distance, they soon fell fast asleep.

55 hazard ['hæzərd] (v.) 遭受危險

🎧(16) Here they were found by Puck, who, seeing a handsome young man asleep, and perceiving that his clothes were made in the Athenian fashion, and that a pretty lady was sleeping near him, concluded that this must be the Athenian maid and her disdainful lover whom Oberon had sent him to seek; and he naturally enough conjectured[56] that, as they were alone together, she must be the first thing he would see when he awoke; so, without more ado[57], he proceeded to pour some of the juice of the little purple flower into his eyes.

But it so fell out, that Helena came that way, and, instead of Hermia, was the first object Lysander beheld when he opened his eyes; and strange to relate, so powerful was the love-charm, all his love for Hermia vanished away, and Lysander fell in love with Helena.

Had he first seen Hermia when he awoke, the blunder Puck committed would have been of no consequence, for he could not love that faithful lady too well.

---

56 conjecture [kən'dʒektʃər] (v.) 猜測；推想
57 ado [ə'duː] (n.) 〔古代用法〕無謂的紛擾

17 But for poor Lysander to be forced by a fairy love-charm, to forget his own true Hermia, and to run after another lady, and leave Hermia asleep quite alone in a wood at midnight, was a sad chance indeed.

Thus this misfortune happened. Helena, as has been before related, endeavored to keep pace with Demetrius when he ran away so rudely from her; but she could not continue this unequal race long, men being always better runners in a long race than ladies. Helena soon lost sight of Demetrius; and as she was wandering about, dejected[58] and forlorn[59], she arrived at the place where Lysander was sleeping.

"Ah!" said she, "this is Lysander lying on the ground: is he dead or asleep?" Then, gently touching him, she said, "Good sir, if you are alive, awake."

Upon this Lysander opened his eyes, and (the love-charm beginning to work) immediately addressed her in terms of extravagant[60] love and admiration; telling her she as much excelled Hermia in beauty as a dove does a raven, and that he would run through fire for her sweet sake; and many more such lover-like speeches.

---

58 dejected [dɪˈdʒektɪd] (a.) 悲傷的;沮喪的
59 forlorn [fərˈlɔːrn] (a.)〔詩的用法〕〔文學用法〕不幸的;孤零的
60 extravagant [ɪkˈstrævəgənt] (a.)(指思想、言論、行為)過分的

Helena. O weary night, O long and tedious night.

18 Helena, knowing Lysander was her friend Hermia's lover, and that he was solemnly engaged to marry her, was in the utmost rage when she heard herself addressed in this manner; for she thought (as well she might) that Lysander was making a jest[61] of her.

"Oh!" said she, "why was I born to be mocked and scorned[62] by every one? Is it not enough, is it not enough, young man, that I can never get a sweet look or a kind word from Demetrius; but you, sir, must pretend in this disdainful manner to court me? I thought, Lysander, you were a lord of more true gentleness."

---

61 jest [dʒest] (n.) 笑柄
62 scorn [skɔːrn] (v.) 輕蔑

Saying these words in great anger, she ran away; and Lysander followed her, quite forgetful of his own Hermia, who was still asleep.

When Hermia awoke, she was in a sad fright[63] at finding herself alone. She wandered about the wood, not knowing what was become of Lysander, or which way to go to seek for him.

In the meantime Demetrius not being able to find Hermia and his rival Lysander, and fatigued with his fruitless search, was observed by Oberon fast asleep. Oberon had learnt by some questions he had asked of Puck, that he had applied the love-charm to the wrong person's eyes; and now having found the person first intended, he touched the eyelids of the sleeping Demetrius with the love-juice, and he instantly awoke; and the first thing he saw being Helena, he, as Lysander had done before, began to address love-speeches to her; and just as that moment Lysander, followed by Hermia (for through Puck's unlucky mistake it was now become Hermia's turn to run after her lover), made his appearance; and then Lysander and Demetrius, both speaking together, made love to Helena, they being each one under the influence of the same potent[64] charm.

---

63 fright [fraɪt] (n.) 驚駭
64 potent ['poʊtənt] (a.) （非用於人或機器）有力的；有效的

Demetrius. Thou runaway, thou coward, art thou fled?

The astonished Helena thought that Demetrius, Lysander, and her once dear friend Hermia, were all in a plot together to make a jest of her.

Hermia was as much surprised as Helena: she knew not why Lysander and Demetrius, who both before loved her, were now become the lovers of Helena; and to Hermia the matter seemed to be no jest.

The ladies, who before had always been the dearest of friends, now fell to high words together.

(21) "Unkind Hermia," said Helena, "it is you who have set Lysander to vex[65] me with mock praises; and your other lover Demetrius, who used almost to spurn[66] me with his foot, have you not bid him call me Goddess, Nymph, rare, precious, and celestial[67]? He would not speak thus to me, whom he hates, if you did not set him on to make a jest of me. Unkind Hermia, to join with men in scorning your poor friend. Have you forgot our school-day friendship? How often, Hermia, have we two, sitting on one cushion, both singing one song, with our needles working the same flower, both on the same sampler wrought[68], growing up together in fashion of a double cherry, scarcely seeming parted! Hermia, it is not friendly in you, it is not maidenly to join with men in scorning your poor friend."

"I am amazed at your passionate words," said Hermia: "I scorn you not; it seems you scorn me."

65 vex [veks] (v.) 使惱怒；苦惱
66 spurn [spɜːrn] (v.) 輕蔑地拒絕
67 celestial [sɪˈlestʃəl] (a.) 極佳的
68 wrought [rɔːt] (a.)〔舊的用法〕製成的（work 的過去式）

(22) "Ay, do," returned Helena, "persevere[69], counterfeit[70] serious looks, and make mouths at me when I turn my back; then wink at each other, and hold the sweet jest up. If you had any pity, grace, or manners, you would not use me thus."

While Helena and Hermia were speaking these angry words to each other, Demetrius and Lysander left them, to fight together in the wood for the love of Helena.

When they found the gentlemen had left them, they departed, and once more wandered weary in the wood in search of their lovers.

69 persevere [ˌpɜːrsɪ'vɪr] (v.) 堅忍；堅持
70 counterfeit ['kaʊntərfɪt] (v.) 偽造；假裝

🎧 23   As soon as they were gone, the fairy king, who with little Puck had been listening to their quarrels, said to him, "This is your negligence, Puck; or did you do this wilfully?"

"Believe me, king of shadows," answered Puck, "it was a mistake; did not you tell me I should know the man by his Athenian garments? However, I am not sorry this has happened, for I think their jangling[71] makes excellent sport."

---

71 jangling [ˈdʒæŋɡəlɪŋ] (n.) 喧鬧的爭論

🎧24 "You heard," said Oberon, "that Demetrius and Lysander are gone to seek a convenient place to fight in. I command you to overhang the night with a thick fog, and lead these quarrelsome lovers so astray in the dark, that they shall not be able to find each other. Counterfeit each of their voices to the other, and with bitter taunts[72] provoke them to follow you, while they think it is their rival's tongue they hear. See you do this, till they are so weary they can go no farther; and when you find they are asleep, drop the juice of this other flower into Lysander's eyes, and when he awakes he will forget his new love for

Helena, and return to his old passion for Hermia; and then the two fair ladies may each one be happy with the man she loves, and they will think all that has passed a vexatious dream. About this quickly, Puck, and I will go and see what sweet love my Titania has found."

---

72 taunt [tɔːnt] (n.) 辱罵

25   Titania was still
sleeping, and Oberon
seeing a clown near
her, who had lost
his way in the wood,
and was likewise
asleep: "This fellow,"
said he, "shall be my
Titania's true love;"
and clapping[73] an ass's
head over the clown's,
it seemed to fit him
as well as if it had
grown upon his own
shoulders.

Though Oberon fixed the ass's head on very gently,
it awakened him, and rising up, unconscious of what
Oberon had done to him, he went towards the bower
where the fairy queen slept.

"Ah! what angel is that I see?" said Titania, opening
her eyes, and the juice of the little purple flower
beginning to take effect: "are you as wise as you are
beautiful?"

73 clap [klæp] (v.) 急速放置

26 "Why, mistress," said the foolish clown, "if I have wit enough to find the way out of this wood, I have enough to serve my turn."

"Out of the wood do not desire to go," said the enamored[74] queen. "I am a spirit of no common rate. I love you. Go with me, and I will give you fairies to attend upon you."

She then called four of her fairies: their names were, Pease-blossom, Cobweb, Moth, and Mustard-seed.

"Attend," said the queen, "upon this sweet gentleman; hop in his walks, and gambol[75] in his sight; feed him with grapes and apricots, and steal for him the honey-bags from the bees. Come, sit with me," said she to the clown, "and let me play with your amiable hairy cheeks, my beautiful ass! and kiss your fair large ears, my gentle joy!"

---

74 enamored [ɪˈnæmərd] (a.) 痴心的
75 gambol [ˈgæmbəl] (v.) 雀躍；嬉戲

🎧 27 "Where is Pease-blossom?" said the ass-headed clown, not much regarding the fairy queen's courtship, but very proud of his new attendants.

"Here, sir," said little Pease-blossom.

"Scratch my head," said the clown. "Where is Cobweb?"

"Here, sir," said Cobweb.

"Good Mr. Cobweb," said the foolish clown, "kill me the red humblebee on the top of that thistle[76] yonder; and, good Mr. Cobweb, bring me the honey-bag. Do not fret[77] yourself too much in the action, Mr. Cobweb, and take care the honey-bag break not; I should be sorry to have you overflown with a honey-bag. Where is Mustard-seed?"

76 thistle ['θɪsl] (n.) （植物）薊
77 fret [frɛt] (v.) 煩惱；煩躁

"Here, sir," said Mustard-seed: "what is your will?"

"Nothing," said the clown, "good Mr. Mustard-seed, but to help Mr. Pease-blossom to scratch; I must go to a barber's, Mr. Mustard-seed, for methinks I am marvelous hairy about the face."

"My sweet love," said the queen, "what will you have to eat? I have a venturous fairy shall seek the squirrel's hoard[78], and fetch you some new nuts."

"I had rather have a handful of dried pease[79]," said the clown, who with his ass's head had got an ass's appetite. "But, I pray, let none of your people disturb me, for I have a mind to sleep."

"Sleep, then," said the queen, "and I will wind you in my arms. O how I love you! how I dote upon you!"

When the fairy king saw the clown sleeping in the arms of his queen, he advanced within her sight, and reproached her with having lavished[80] her favors upon an ass.

This she could not deny, as the clown was then sleeping within her arms, with his ass's head crowned by her with flowers.

---

78 hoard [hɔːrd] (n.) 節省下來妥善保存的食物
79 pease [piːz] (n.) 〔已廢棄的用法〕豌豆
80 lavish ['lævɪʃ] (v.) 慷慨贈與

TITANIA.
Out of this wood do not desire to go:
Thou shalt remain here, whether thou wilt or no.
I am a spirit of no common rate.

When Oberon had teased her for some time, he again demanded the changeling boy; which she, ashamed of being discovered by her lord with her new favorite, did not dare to refuse him.

Oberon, having thus obtained the little boy he had so long wished for to be his page, took pity on the disgraceful situation into which, by his merry contrivance, he had brought his Titania, and threw some of the juice of the other flower into her eyes; and the fairy queen immediately recovered her senses, and wondered at her late dotage, saying how she now loathed[81] the sight of the strange monster.

Oberon likewise took the ass's head from off the clown, and left him to finish his nap with his own fool's head upon his shoulders.

Oberon and his Titania being now perfectly reconciled[82], he related to her the history of the lovers, and their midnight quarrels; and she agreed to go with him and see the end of their adventures.

---

81 loathe [louð] (v.) 厭惡
82 reconcile ['rekənsaɪl] (v.) 爭吵後和好；和解

The fairy king and queen found the lovers and their fair ladies, at no great distance from each other, sleeping on a grass-plot; for Puck, to make amends[83] for his former mistake, had contrived with the utmost diligence[84] to bring them all to the same spot, unknown to each other; and he had carefully removed the charm from off the eyes of Lysander with the antidote[85] the fairy king gave to him.

83 amends [ə'mendz] (n.)（用複數形）補償
84 diligence ['dɪlədʒəns] (n.) 勤勉
85 antidote ['æntɪdoʊt] (n.) 解藥；抗毒劑

Hermia first awoke, and finding her lost Lysander asleep so near her, was looking at him and wondering at his strange inconstancy. Lysander presently opening his eyes, and seeing his dear Hermia, recovered his reason which the fairy charm had before clouded, and with his reason, his love for Hermia; and they began to talk over the adventures of the night, doubting if these things had really happened, or if they had both been dreaming the same bewildering[86] dream.

Helena and Demetrius were by this time awake; and a sweet sleep having quieted Helena's disturbed and angry spirits, she listened with delight to the professions of love which Demetrius still made to her, and which, to her surprise as well as pleasure, she began to perceive were sincere.

---

86 bewildering [bɪˈwɪldərɪŋ] (a.) 迷惑的；手足無措的

🎧 **32** These fair night-wandering ladies, now no longer rivals, became once more true friends; all the unkind words which had passed were forgiven, and they calmly consulted together what was best to be done in their present situation. It was soon agreed that, as Demetrius had given up his pretensions[87] to Hermia, he should endeavor to prevail upon her father to revoke[88] the cruel sentence of death which had been passed against her. Demetrius was preparing to return to Athens for this friendly purpose, when they were surprised with the sight of Egeus, Hermia's father, who came to the wood in pursuit of his runaway daughter.

When Egeus understood that Demetrius would not now marry his daughter, he no longer opposed her marriage with Lysander, but gave his consent that they should be wedded on the fourth day from that time, being the same day on which Hermia had been condemned[89] to lose her life; and on that same day Helena joyfully agreed to marry her beloved and now faithful Demetrius.

87 pretensions [prɪˈtenʃənz] (n.)（常用複數形）主張
88 revoke [rɪˈvoʊk] (v.) 撤銷；取消
89 condemn [kənˈdem] (v.) 判罪；處刑

🎧33 The fairy king and queen, who were invisible spectators of this reconciliation, and now saw the happy ending of the lovers' history, brought about through the good offices[90] of Oberon, received so much pleasure, that these kind spirits resolved to celebrate the approaching nuptials[91] with sports and revels throughout their fairy kingdom.

90 offices ['ɔːfɪsəs] (n.)（複數形）殷勤；服務
91 nuptials ['nʌpʃəlz] (n.)（複數形）婚禮

🎧 34 And now, if any are offended with this story of fairies and their pranks, as judging it incredible and strange, they have only to think that they have been asleep and dreaming, and that all these adventures were visions which they saw in their sleep; and I hope none of my readers will be so unreasonable as to be offended with a pretty harmless Midsummer Night's Dream.

The End

Lysander The course of true love never did run smooth;
But, either it was different in blood —

Hermia O cross! too high to be enthrall'd to low.

Lysander Or else misgraffed in respect of years —

Hermia O spite! too old to be engag'd to young.

Lysander Or else it stood upon the choice of friends, —

Hermia O hell! to choose love by another's eye.
(I, i, 134-40)

萊桑德 真愛之路永崎嶇；
若非血統有差異——

荷米雅 不幸啊，身分懸殊難屈就！

萊桑德 便是年齡難以嫁接——

荷米雅 可惜啊，老少如何能婚配！

萊桑德 或聽憑友人之選擇——

荷米雅 倒楣啊，得憑外人眼光擇愛人！
（第一幕，第一景，134-40 行）

Puck   Captain of our fairy band,
          Helena is here at hand,
          And the youth, mistook by me,
          Pleading for a lover's fee.
          Shall we their fond pageant see?
          Lord, what fools these mortals be!
          (III, ii, 110-15)

帕克   呈報仙界之首腦，
        已經帶來海蓮娜，
        身後隨來少年郎，
        苦苦哀求她憋憐。
        瞧那癡戀的模樣，
        愚蠢凡人無法想！
        （第三幕，第二景，110-15 行）

As You Like It

皆大歡喜

導讀

歡慶喜劇

《皆大歡喜》一般推測的寫作年代為 1599-1600 年，此劇通常與《無事生非》及《第十二夜》並列為莎士比亞的三大歡慶喜劇（festive comedy）。

本劇有若干常見的莎劇主題，例如：由宮廷城市進入原始森林（如《仲夏夜之夢》）、善惡對比的兩兄弟（如《暴風雨》）、女扮男裝（如《威尼斯商人》、《第十二夜》）等。

本故事的來源有二，一是勞巨（Thomas Lodge）在 1590 年出版且大受歡迎的《羅瑟琳》（Rosalynde），二是中古時期著名的暴力劇《嘉米林的故事》（The Tale of Gamelyn）。前者描寫田園生活中的浪漫愛情故事，後者描述弟弟如何向苛待他的兄長復仇。

《皆大歡喜》改寫當中的諸多情節，焦點放在羅莎琳與歐藍多的戀情，結局溫和。本劇劇情進展迅速，對白和情境環繞田園生活和愛情故事。全劇的手法強調「內容重於語言，語言重於情節」，所以劇中並沒有任何懸疑或明顯的衝突。劇末，所有的恩怨情仇都奇蹟似的被化解掉，最後結束流亡生涯，重返宮廷。

「命」與「運」

文藝復興時期的英國偏向從「命」（nature）和「運」（fortune）的互動來詮釋生命。《皆》劇中唯一令人感到緊張不安的，是惡劣運勢使得正義難以伸張，好人受苦，壞人享樂。

莎翁的戲劇通常呈現多元的主題和複雜的心理層面，人物性格通常好壞善惡兼雜，其所表現的戲劇張力，也有許多是源於內心欲望與外在命運的相互衝突。但本劇解決「命」與「運」之衝突的方法卻教人啞然失笑：兩個反派角色最後痛改前非，搖身一變成為好人。天性邪惡的人只因「運」巧逢善人指導，從此悔過向善，因此沒有受到懲罰。

田園文學

本劇的獨特點之一是椏藤森林，讓全劇充滿濃厚的田園文學氣息。椏藤森林的名稱可能源於莎翁故鄉瓦維克（Warwick）附近的一個城鎮，這也是他母親瑪麗・椏藤（Mary Arden）的姓氏，也有可能是直接取用《羅瑟琳》中的地名阿登（Ardenne，這個法文就是英文的Arden）。

在概念上，椏藤森林則可能類似俠盜羅賓漢的「雪梧森林」（Sherwood Forest），也可能是《聖經》裡的「伊甸園」，或是文學傳統裡的田野「雅卡迪」（Acardia）。這些地點象徵對理想世界的憧憬及嚮往。傳統的田園文學作品都將原野描寫為靜謐祥和之地，是遠離城鎮宮廷的庇護所。

AS YOU LIKE IT

這種文學傳統始於古希臘詩人希奧奎底斯（Theocrites）對鄉野的謳歌，古羅馬詩人維吉爾（Virgil）延續此風格，強調田園生活與都市生活的對比。

到了文藝復興時期，就演變為鄉村與都市互相敵對的狀態。不少與莎翁同期的作家也曾依循這項傳統，其中較為著名的就是史賓塞（Edmund Spenser）和席德尼爵士（Sir Philip Sidney）。

田園與城市的相對性

在典型的田園文學作品中，常可見到主人翁從城都或宮廷中遭放逐的情節。這些被放逐的人在重返故城之前，都會經歷一番閒適無爭的田園生活，並喜歡上此一生活方式，而自視為牧羊人。作品中常出現歌唱和討論，其中常見的討論內容如：鄉村與都市生活的優缺點；人類的藝術，究竟是美化還是破壞了自然？高貴的天性，是與生俱來還是後天培養而成？這些辯論的核心在於自然與人為的關係，亦即城市、制度、社會階級等，是否優於簡單純樸的自然景致。

也因為盛行這種討論，使得田園文學漸漸轉向社會批評。莎翁在《皆》劇中則同時表現了對田園文學的認同與批評。雖然劇中人最後在椏藤森林得到重生，但其原因並不只是靠大自然治癒心靈的力量，人類的善良和慷慨也佔有很大的成分。因此，除了自然的陶冶，人類也需要文明的教化，愛情、寬容、幽默、智慧等須和大自然互相結合，才能臻於和諧。

成熟的女主角

歐藍多出場時,是個天性高貴的純樸青年,但因不曉人事而參加角力賽。另一個顯示他人生閱歷不足的地方,是他在林樹上到處刻著書本上讀來的十四行詩,這僅表現其純情癡心,卻不能代表他了解愛情。他必須等到羅莎琳出現,才能邁向更成熟階段。

羅莎琳就像許多莎劇的女主角一樣(如茱麗葉、《威尼斯商人》的波兒榭、《終成眷屬》的海倫娜),在心智與感情上都比情人成熟。羅莎琳採取理智務實的態度,使歐藍多避免陷入佩脫拉克式戀情的窠臼,其主要特徵是以誇大而不著邊際的方式,歌頌詩人心目中完美的理想情人,而事實上卻沒有真正獲得心上人的回應。

羅莎琳是莎劇中最生動迷人的女主角之一。她是本劇中的第一女主角,卻大都以男性裝扮出現,就像波兒榭與《第十二夜》的菲兒拉一樣。她們之所以女扮男裝,主要是藉以避免危險、自我保護、追求愛情,或是取得社會中具有權力的性別地位。(但我們也不要忘記當時的女性角色一律由少年扮演,因此莎士比亞創造這些劇情,可說是因應社會風俗及演員特質的特殊安排。)

在這幾個女扮男裝的例子中,羅莎琳是最為複雜的一個。文藝復興時期的女孩在家順從父母,嫁出去之後順從丈夫。但羅莎琳因父親被放逐,叔叔又把她趕出宮外,所以她沒有男性監護人,凡事必須自立。另外,她雖女扮男裝,但仍擁有「典型」的女性特質,例如對瑟梨兒坦承她愛上歐藍多,或是聽到歐藍多受傷後就馬上昏厥等等。

雌雄莫辨的議題

文藝復興時期的劇場傳統，更讓這種雌雄莫辨呈現萬花筒式的鏡像關係。她原由少男所飾演，卻必須在劇中化身為名叫嘉尼米的男性，爾後再還原為女性羅莎琳，而觀眾還是不會忘記她原是由「他」所扮演。（文藝復興時期受到希臘醫學的影響，認為男女的性特徵並沒有很大的差異，因此主要是從服裝及舉止上來辨別男女。）

羅莎琳化身成男性嘉尼米，凸顯了性別轉換和同性戀的議題。嘉尼米是希臘神話中同性戀的代表人物，在文藝復興時期則象徵年長男子的少年情人。或許有人會將嘉尼米與歐藍多的感情詮釋為同性戀，而且田園文學中也早有歌頌同性戀的傳統。史賓塞在《牧羊年曆》（The Shepheardes Calendar）中就有類似的情節，而在 1580 年代的《深情牧羊人》（The Affectionate Shepherd）中，男主人翁更是大方地表白自己對年輕男子嘉尼米的愛意。

嘉尼米和歐藍多之間的情誼是否為同性戀，見仁見智。有些批評家認為，嘉尼米其實是提供歐藍多認識羅莎琳的階梯，讓他先從嘉尼米身上獲得同性友誼，待建立彼此信任的關係後，再進一步從羅莎琳身上獲得異性的愛情。就劇本的角度來看，也的確如此，但若以當時角色扮演的性別限制，還有莎士比亞選擇了嘉尼米這個名字來看，恐怕就沒有那麼單純了。

一般的評價

自十八世紀起，評論家似乎都認為《皆大歡喜》的寫作技巧並不好。英國作家強生（Samuel Johnson）認為此劇的結局過於匆促，失去陳述道德教育的機會；愛爾蘭劇作家蕭伯納（George Bernard Shaw, 1856-1950）半開玩笑地表示，這個劇本不過是剽竊通俗故事裡的劇情，所謂的「皆大歡喜」（As You Like It）不過是「皆我（莎士比亞）喜歡」（as I like it）罷了；英國導演布魯克（Peter Brook）看完此劇文本後，也向莎士比亞說「我不喜歡」（as I don't like it）；也有人認為此劇前後矛盾，而且許多問題到劇終時仍然沒有獲得解決。

本劇在莎士比亞死後一直到 1740 年才開始有演出紀錄，之後逐漸成為莎劇的常備劇目。十九世紀末，此劇移至戶外公演後，更是經常呈現圖畫般的景象。到了二十世紀，本劇因為同時呈現純真與嘲諷、浪漫與寫實，而同時吸引了喜好知識與夢想的觀眾。

人物表

the duck	流放公爵	一位被弟弟篡位而被流放到森林裡的公爵
Rosalind	羅莎琳	公爵的獨生女，後男扮女裝，化名嘉尼米（Ganymede）
Celia	瑟梨兒	費得烈公爵的女兒，後喬裝村姑，化名雅菱娜（Aliena）
Orlando	歐藍多	貴族出身，和羅莎琳邂逅相戀
Duke Frederick	費得烈公爵	逐兄篡位，流放公爵的弟弟
Oliver	歐力維	歐藍多的兄長，待弟甚苛
Adam	亞當	歐藍多忠實的老僕人

As You Like It

During the time that France was divided into provinces (or dukedoms[1], as they were called) there reigned in one of these provinces a usurper[2] who had deposed[3] and banished his elder brother, the lawful duke.

The duke who was thus driven from his dominions retired with a few faithful followers to the forest of Arden; and here the good duke lived with his loving friends, who had put themselves into a voluntary exile for his sake, while their land and revenues enriched the false usurper; and custom soon made the life of careless ease they led here more sweet to them than the pomp and uneasy splendor of a courtier's life.

Here they lived like the old Robin Hood of England, and to this forest many noble youths daily resorted[4] from the court, and did fleet the time carelessly, as they did who lived in the golden age. In the summer they lay along under the fine shade of the large forest trees, marking the playful sports of the wild deer; and so fond were they of these poor dappled[5] fools, who seemed to be the native inhabitants of the forest, that it grieved them to be forced to kill them to supply themselves with venison[6] for their food.

---

1 dukedom ['duːkdəm] (n.) 公國
2 usurper [juːˈzɜːrpər] (n.) 篡奪者；霸占者
3 depose [dɪˈpouz] (v.) 迫使下台
4 resort [rɪˈzɔːrt] (v.) 常去
5 dappled ['dæpəld] (a.) 斑紋的
6 venison ['venɪsən] (n.) 鹿肉

When the cold winds of winter made the duke feel the change of his adverse fortune, he would endure it patiently, and say: "These chilling winds which blow upon my body are true counselors; they do not flatter, but represent truly to me my condition; and though they bite sharply, their tooth is nothing like so keen as that of unkindness and ingratitude. I find that howsoever men speak against adversity[7], yet some sweet uses are to be extracted[8] from it; like the jewel, cious for medicine, which is taken from the head of the venomous[9] and despised toad."

7 adversity [ədˈvɜːrsɪti] (n.) 厄運；災難
8 extract [ɪkˈstrækt] (v.) 拔出
9 venomous [ˈvenəməs] (a.) 有毒的

🎧 37 In this manner did the patient duke draw a useful moral from everything that he saw; and by the help of this moralizing turn, in that life of his, remote from public haunts, he could find tongues in trees, books in the running brooks, sermons[10] in stones, and good in everything.

The banished duke had an only daughter, named Rosalind, whom the usurper, Duke Frederick, when he banished her father, still retained in his court as a companion for his own daughter, Celia. A strict friendship subsisted[11] between these ladies, which the disagreement between their fathers did not in the least interrupt, Celia striving by every kindness in her power to make amends to Rosalind for the injustice of her own father in deposing the father of Rosalind; and whenever the thoughts of her father's banishment, and her own dependence on the false usurper, made Rosalind melancholy, Celia's whole care was to comfort and console her.

10 sermon ['sɜːrmən] (n.) 說教
11 subsist [səb'sɪst] (v.) 存在

 One day, when Celia was talking in her usual kind manner to Rosalind, saying, "I pray you, Rosalind, my sweet cousin, be merry," a messenger entered from the duke, to tell them that if they wished to see a wrestling-match, which was just going to begin, they must come instantly to the court before the palace; and Celia, thinking it would amuse Rosalind, agreed to go and see it.

In those times wrestling, which is only practised now by country clowns, was a favorite sport even in the courts of princes, and before fair ladies and princesses. To this wrestling-match, therefore, Celia and Rosalind went.

🎧 **39**   They found that it was likely to prove a very tragical sight; for a large and powerful man, who had been long practised in the art of wrestling and had slain many men in contests of this kind, was just going to wrestle with a very young man, who, from his extreme youth and inexperience in the art, the beholders all thought would certainly be killed.

When the duke saw Celia and Rosalind he said: "How now, daughter and niece, are you crept hither to see the wrestling? You will take little delight in it, there is such odds in the men. In pity to this young man, I would wish to persuade him from wrestling. Speak to him, ladies, and see if you can move him."

The ladies were well pleased to perform this humane office, and first Celia entreated the young stranger that he would desist from the attempt; and then Rosalind spoke so kindly to him, and with such feeling consideration for the danger he was about to undergo, that, instead of being persuaded by her gentle words to forego his purpose, all his thoughts were bent to distinguish himself by his courage in this lovely lady's eyes.

🎧 40 He refused the request of Celia and Rosalind in such graceful and modest words that they felt still more concern for him; he concluded his refusal with saying: "I am sorry to deny such fair and excellent ladies anything. But let your fair eyes and gentle wishes go with me to my trial, wherein if I be conquered there is one shamed that was never gracious; if I am killed, there is one dead that is willing to die. I shall do my friends no wrong, for I have none to lament me; the world no injury, for in it I have nothing; for I only fill up a place in the world which may be better supplied when I have made it empty."

And now the wrestling-match began. Celia wished the young stranger might not be hurt; but Rosalind felt most for him. The friendless state which he said he was in, and that he wished to die, made Rosalind think that he was, like herself, unfortunate; and she pitied him so much, and so deep an interest she took in his danger while he was wrestling, that she might almost be said at that moment to have fallen in love with him.

The kindness shown this unknown youth by these fair and noble ladies gave him courage and strength, so that he performed wonders; and in the end completely conquered his antagonist, who was so much hurt that for a while he was unable to speak or move.

🎧 42 The Duke Frederick was much pleased with the courage and skill shown by this young stranger; and desired to know his name and parentage, meaning to take him under his protection.

The stranger said his name was Orlando, and that he was the youngest son of Sir Rowland de Boys.

Sir Rowland de Boys, the father of Orlando, had been dead some years; but when he was living he had been a true subject and dear friend of the banished duke; therefore, when Frederick heard Orlando was the son of his banished brother's friend, all his liking for this brave young man was changed into displeasure and he left the place in very ill humor. Hating to bear the very name of any of his brother's friends, and yet still admiring the valor of the youth, he said, as he went out, that he wished Orlando had been the son of any other man.

Rosalind was delighted to hear that her new favorite was the son of her father's old friend; and she said to Celia, "My father loved Sir Rowland de Boys, and if I had known this young man was his son I would have added tears to my entreaties before he should have ventured."

🎧 43 The ladies then went up to him and, seeing him abashed[12] by the sudden displeasure shown by the duke, they spoke kind and encouraging words to him; and Rosalind, when they were going away, turned back to speak some more civil things to the brave young son of her father's old friend, and taking a chain from off her neck, she said: "Gentleman, wear this for me. I am out of suits with fortune, or I would give you a more valuable present."

When the ladies were alone, Rosalind's talk being still of Orlando, Celia began to perceive her cousin had fallen in love with the handsome young wrestler, and she said to Rosalind: "Is it possible you should fall in love so suddenly?"

Rosalind replied, "The duke, my father, loved his father dearly."

"But," said Celia, "does it therefore follow that you should love his son dearly?. For then I ought to hate him, for my father hated his father; yet do not hate Orlando."

12 abash [ə'bæʃ] (v.) 使羞愧不安

🎧 Frederick, being enraged at the sight of Sir Rowland de Boys's son, which reminded him of the many friends the banished duke had among the nobility, and having been for some time displeased with his niece because the people praised her for her virtues and pitied her for her good father's sake, his malice[13] suddenly broke out against her; and while Celia and Rosalind were talking of Orlando, Frederick entered the room and with looks full of anger ordered Rosalind instantly to leave the palace and follow her father into banishment, telling Celia, who in vain pleaded for her, that he had only suffered Rosalind to stay upon her account.

"I did not then," said Celia, "entreat you to let her stay, for I was too young at that time to value her; but now that I know her worth, and that we so long have slept together, rose at the same instant, learned, played, and eat together, I cannot live out of her company."

Frederick replied, "She is too subtle for you; her smoothness, her very silence, and her patience speak to the people, and they pity her. You are a fool to plead for her, for you will seem more bright and virtuous when she is gone; therefore open not your lips in her favor, for the doom which I have passed upon her is irrevocable[14]."

13 malice ['mælɪs] (n.) 惡意
14 irrevocable [ɪ'revəkəbəl] (a.) 不可挽回的

Celia

45 When Celia found she could not prevail upon her father to let Rosalind remain with her, she generously resolved to accompany her; and, leaving her father's palace that night, she went along with her friend to seek Rosalind's father, the banished duke, in the forest of Arden.

Before they set out Celia considered that it would be unsafe for two young ladies to travel in the rich clothes they then wore; she therefore proposed that they should disguise their rank by dressing themselves like country maids. Rosalind said it would be a still greater protection if one of them was to be dressed like a man. And so it was quickly agreed on between them that, as Rosalind was the tallest, she should wear the dress of a young countryman, and Celia should be habited like a country lass, and that they should say they were brother and sister; and Rosalind said she would be called Ganymede, and Celia chose the name of Aliena.

In this disguise, and taking their money and jewels to defray[15] their expenses, these fair princesses set out on their long travel; for the forest of Arden was a long way off, beyond the boundaries of the duke's dominions.

15 defray [dɪ'freɪ] (v.) 支付

Ganymede

🎧 The lady Rosalind (or Ganymede, as she must now be called) with her manly garb seemed to have put on a manly courage. The faithful friendship Celia had shown in accompanying Rosalind so many weary miles made the new brother, in recompense[16] for this true love, exert a cheerful spirit, as if he were indeed Ganymede, the rustic and stout[17]-hearted brother of the gentle village maiden, Aliena.

When at last they came to the forest of Arden they no longer found the convenient inns and good accommodations they had met with on the road, and, being in want of food and rest, Ganymede, who had so merrily cheered his sister with pleasant speeches and happy remarks all the way, now owned to Aliena that he was so weary he could find in his heart to disgrace his man's apparel[18] and cry like a woman; and Aliena declared she could go no farther; and then again Ganymede tried to recollect that it was a man's duty to comfort and console a woman, as the weaker vessel[19], and to seem courageous to his new sister, he said: "Come, have a good heart, my sister Aliena. We are now at the end of our travel, in the forest of Arden."

---

16 recompense ['rekəmpens] (n.) 報償
17 stout [staʊt] (a.) 堅決的；剛毅的
18 apparel [ə'pærəl] (n.) 服裝
19 vessel ['vesəl] (n.) 血管

(47) But feigned manliness and forced courage would no longer support them; for, though they were in the forest of Arden, they knew not where to find the duke. And here the travel of these weary ladies might have come to a sad conclusion, for they might have lost themselves and perished for want of

food, but, providentially, as they were sitting on the grass, almost dying with fatigue and hopeless of any relief, a countryman chanced to pass that way, and Ganymede once more tried to speak with a manly boldness, saying: "Shepherd, if love or gold can in this desert place procure[20] us entertainment[21], I pray you bring us where we may rest ourselves; for this young maid, my sister, is much fatigued with traveling, and faints for want of food."

[20] procure [proʊˈkjʊr] (v.) 促成；招致
[21] entertainment [ˌentərˈteɪnmənt] (n.) 飲食

🎧 48 The man replied that he was only a servant to a shepherd, and that his master's house was just going to be sold, and therefore they would find but poor entertainment; but that if they would go with him they should be welcome to what there was.

They followed the man, the near prospect of relief giving them fresh strength, and bought the house and sheep of the shepherd, and took the man who conducted them to the shepherd's house to wait on them; and being by this means so fortunately provided with a neat cottage, and well supplied with provisions[22], they agreed to stay here till they could learn in what part of the forest the duke dwelt.

When they were rested after the fatigue of their journey, they began to like their new way of life, and almost fancied themselves the shepherd and shepherdess they feigned to be. Yet sometimes Ganymede remembered be had once been the same Lady Rosalind who had so dearly loved the brave Orlando because be was the son of old Sir Rowland, her father's friend; and though Ganymede thought that Orlando was many miles distant, even so many weary miles as they had traveled, yet it soon appeared that Orlando was also in the forest of Arden. And in this manner this strange event came to pass.

22 provisions [prəˈvɪʒənz] (n.) （作複數形）食物供應

 Orlando was the youngest son of Sir Rowland de Boys, who, when he died, left him (Orlando being then very young) to the care of his eldest brother, Oliver, charging Oliver on his blessing to give his brother a good education and provide for him as became the dignity of their ancient house. Oliver proved an unworthy brother, and, disregarding the commands of his dying father, he never put his brother to school, but kept him at home untaught and entirely neglected.

50   But in his nature and in the noble qualities of his mind Orlando so much resembled his excellent father that, without any advantages of education, he seemed like a youth who had been bred with the utmost care; and Oliver so envied the fine person and dignified manners of his untutored brother that at last he wished to destroy him, and to effect this be set on people to persuade him to wrestle with the famous wrestler who, as has been before related, had killed so many men. Now it was this cruel brother's neglect of him which made Orlando say he wished to die, being so friendless.

When, contrary to the wicked hopes he had formed, his brother proved victorious, his envy and malice knew no bounds, and he swore he would burn the chamber where Orlando slept. He was overheard making his vow by one that had been an old and faithful servant to their father, and that loved Orlando because he resembled Sir Rowland. This old man went out to meet him when he returned from the duke's palace, and when he saw Orlando the peril his dear young master was in made him break out into these passionate exclamations:

"O my gentle master, my sweet master! O you memory of Old Sir Rowland! Why are you virtuous? Why are you gentle, strong, and valiant[23]? And why would you be so fond to overcome the famous wrestler? Your praise is come too swiftly home before you."

Orlando, wondering what all this meant, asked him what was the matter. And then the old man told him how his wicked brother, envying the love all people bore him, and now hearing the fame he had gained by his victory in the duke's palace, intended to destroy him by setting fire to his chamber that night, and in conclusion advised him to escape the danger he was in by instant flight; and knowing Orlando had no money, Adam (for that was the good old man's name) had brought out with him his own little hoard[24], and he said: "I have five hundred crowns, the thrifty[25] hire I saved under your father and laid by to be provision for me when my old limbs should become unfit for service. Take that, and He that doth the ravens feed be comfort to my age! Here is the gold. All this I give to you. Let me be your servant; though I look old I will do the service of a younger man in all your business and necessities."

23 valiant ['væliənt] (a.) 勇敢的
24 hoard [hɔːrd] (n.) 貯藏的錢財
25 thrifty ['θrɪfti] (a.) 節儉的

"O good old man!" said Orlando, "how well appears in you the constant service of the old world! You are not for the fashion of these times. We will go along together, and before your youthful wages are spent I shall light upon some means for both our maintenance."

Together, then, this faithful servant and his loved master set out; and Orlando and Adam traveled on, uncertain what course to pursue, till they came to the forest of Arden, and there they found themselves in the same distress for want of food that Ganymede and Aliena had been. They wandered on, seeking some human habitation, till they were almost spent with hunger and fatigue.

Adam at last said: "O my dear master, I die for want of food. I can go no farther!" He then laid himself down, thinking to make that place his grave, and bade his dear master farewell.

Orlando, seeing him in this weak state, took his old servant up in his arms and carried him under the shelter of some pleasant trees; and he said to him: "Cheerly, old Adam. Rest your weary limbs here awhile, and do not talk of dying!"

Orlando and Adam.

AS YOU LIKE IT.
See my side be comfortable

Orlando then searched about to find some food, and he happened to arrive at that part of the forest where the duke was; and he and his friends were just going to eat their dinner, this royal duke being seated on the grass, under no other canopy[26] than the shady covert[27] of some large trees.

Orlando, whom hunger had made desperate, drew his sword, intending to take their meat by force, and said: "Forbear[28] and eat no more. I must have your food!"

The duke asked him if distress had made him so bold or if he were a rude despiser of good manners.

On this Orlando said he was dying with hunger; and then the duke told him he was welcome to sit down and eat with them.

26 canopy ['kænəpi] (n.) 頂篷
27 covert ['kʌuvərt] (n.) 動物藏身的樹叢
28 forbear ['fɔːrber] (v.) 抑制；忍耐

Orlando, hearing him speak so gently, put up his sword and blushed with shame at the rude manner in which he had demanded their food.

"Pardon me, I pray you," said he. "I thought that all things had been savage here, and therefore I put on the countenance of stern command; but whatever men you are that in this desert, under the shade of melancholy boughs, lose and neglect the creeping hours of time, if ever you have looked on better days, if ever you have been where bells have knolled to church, if you have ever sat at any good man's feast, if ever from your eyelids you have wiped a tear and know what it is to pity or be pitied, may gentle speeches now move you to do me human courtesy!"

The duke replied: "True it is that we are men (as you say) who have seen better days, and though we have now our habitation in this wild forest, we have lived in towns and cities and have with holy bell been knolled to church, have sat at good men's feasts, and from our eyes have wiped the drops which sacred pity has engendered[29], therefore sit you down and take of our refreshment[30] as much as will minister to your wants."

---

29 engender [ɪnˈdʒendər] (v.) 使産生；引起
30 refreshment [rɪˈfreʃmənt] (n.) 提神的東西（尤指食物和飲料）

"There is an old poor man," answered Orlando, "who has limped after me many a weary step in pure love, oppressed at once with two sad infirmities[31], age and hunger; till he be satisfied I must not touch a bit."

"Go, find him out and bring him hither," said the duke. "We will forbear to eat till you return."

Then Orlando went like a doe[32] to find its fawn[33] and give it food; and presently returned, bringing Adam in his arms.

And the duke said, "Set down your venerable[34] burthen[35], you are both welcome."

And they fed the old man and cheered his heart, and he revived and recovered his health and strength again.

The duke inquired who Orlando was; and when he found that he was the son of his old friend, Sir Rowland de Boys, be took him under his protection, and Orlando and his old servant lived with the duke in the forest.

31 infirmity [ɪnˈfɜːrmɪti] (n.) 疾病；弱點
32 doe [doʊ] (n.) 母鹿；雌兔
33 fawn [fɑːn] (n.) 麑；幼小梅花鹿
34 venerable [ˈvenərəbəl] (a.) 可敬的
35 burthen [ˈbɜːrðən] (n.) 〔文學用法〕負擔

ORLANDO. I thank you most for him.
ADAM.   So had you need:
              I scarce can speak to thank you for mysef.

Rosalind & Celia

Orlando arrived in the forest not many days after Ganymede and Aliena came there and (as has been before related) bought the shepherd's cottage.

Ganymede and Aliena were strangely surprised to find the name of Rosalind carved on the trees, and love-sonnets fastened to them, all addressed to Rosalind; and while they were wondering how this could be they met Orlando and they perceived the chain which Rosalind had given him about his neck.

🎧 57 Orlando little thought that Ganymede was the fair Princess Rosalind who, by her noble condescension[36] and favor, had so won his heart that he passed his whole time in carving her name upon the trees and writing sonnets in praise of her beauty; but being much pleased with the graceful air of this pretty shepherd-youth, he entered into conversation with him, and be thought he saw a likeness in Ganymede to his beloved Rosalind, but that he had none of the dignified deportment[37] of that noble lady; for Ganymede assumed the forward[38] manners often seen in youths when they are between boys and men, and with much archness[39] and humor talked to Orlando of a certain lover, "who," said she, "haunts our forest, and spoils our young trees with carving Rosalind upon their barks; and he hangs odes upon hawthorns[40], and elegies[41] on brambles[42], all praising this same Rosalind. If I could find this lover, I would give him some good counsel that would soon cure him of his love."

36 condescension [ˌkɑːndɪˈsenʃən] (n.) 屈尊俯就
37 deportment [dɪˈpɔːrtmənt] (n.) 行為舉止
38 forward [ˈfɔːrwərd] (a.) 魯莽的；冒失的
39 archness [ˈɑːrtʃnəs] (n.) 淘氣
40 hawthorn [ˈhɑːθɔːrn] (n.) 山楂
41 elegy [ˈelɪdʒi] (n.) 哀歌
42 bramble [ˈbræmbəl] (n.) 荊棘

Orlando confessed that he was the fond lover
of whom he spoke,, and asked Ganymede to give
him the good counsel he talked Of. The remedy
Ganymede proposed, and the counsel he gave him
was that Orlando should come every day to the
cottage where he and his sister Aliena dwelt. "And
then," said Ganymede, "I will feign myself to be
Rosalind, and you shall feign to court me in the same
manner as you would do if I was Rosalind, and then I
will imitate the fantastic ways of whimsical[43] ladies to
their lovers, till I make you ashamed of your love; and
this is the way I propose to cure you."

Orlando had no great faith in the remedy, yet he
agreed to come every day to Ganymede's cottage
and feign a playful courtship; and every day Orlando
visited Ganymede and Aliena, and Orlando called
the shepherd Ganymede his Rosalind, and every
day talked over all the fine words and flattering
compliments which young men delight to use when
they court their mistresses. It does not appear,
however, that Ganymede made any progress in curing
Orlando of his love for Rosalind.

43 whimsical ['wɪmzɪkəl] (a.) 異想天開的

59 Though Orlando thought all this was but a sportive play (not dreaming that Ganymede was his very Rosalind), yet the opportunity it gave him of saying all the fond things he had in his heart pleased his fancy almost as well as it did Ganymede's, who enjoyed the secret jest in knowing these fine love-speeches were all addressed to the right person.

In this manner many days passed pleasantly on with these young people; and the good-natured Aliena, seeing it made Ganymede happy, let him have his own way and was diverted at the mock-courtship, and did not care to remind Ganymede that the Lady Rosalind had not yet made herself known to the duke her father, whose place of resort in the forest they had learned from Orlando.

🎧 60 Ganymede met the duke one day, and had some talk with him, and the duke asked of what parentage he came. Ganymede answered that he came of as good parentage as he did, which made the duke smile, for he did not suspect the pretty shepherd-boy came of royal lineage[44]. Then seeing the duke look well and happy, Ganymede was content to put off all further explanation for a few days longer.

One morning, as Orlando was going to visit Ganymede, he saw a man lying asleep on the ground, and a large green snake had twisted itself about his neck. The snake, seeing Orlando approach, glided[45] away among the bushes. Orlando went nearer, and then he discovered a lioness lie crouching[46], with her head on the ground, with a catlike watch, waiting until the sleeping man awaked (for it is said that lions will prey on nothing that is dead or sleeping).

---

44 lineage ['lɪnɪɪdʒ] (n.) 世系；血統
45 glide [glaɪd] (v.) 滑行
46 crouch [krautʃ] (v.) 蹲伏

[61]   It seemed as if Orlando was sent by Providence[47] to free the man from the danger of the snake and lioness; but when Orlando looked in the man's face he perceived that the sleeper who was exposed to this double peril was his own brother Oliver, who had so cruelly used him and had threatened to destroy him by fire, and he was almost tempted to leave him a prey[48] to the hungry lioness; but brotherly affection and the gentleness of his nature soon overcame his first anger against his brother; and he drew his sword and attacked the lioness and slew her, and thus preserved his brother's life both from the venomous snake and from the furious lioness; but before Orlando could conquer the lioness she had torn one of his arms with her sharp claws.

47 Providence [ˈprɑːvɪdəns] (n.) ﹙作大寫﹚神；上帝
48 prey [preɪ] (n.) 被捕食的動物

While Orlando was engaged with the lioness, Oliver awaked, and, perceiving that his brother Orlando, whom he had so cruelly treated, was saving him from the fury of a wild beast at the risk of his own life, shame and remorse[49] at once seized him, and he repented[50] of his unworthy conduct and besought with many tears his brother's pardon for the injuries he had done him. Orlando rejoiced to see him so penitent[51], and readily forgave him. They embraced each other and from that hour Oliver loved Orlando with a true brotherly affection, though he had come to the forest bent on his destruction.

The wound in Orlando's arm having bled very much, he found himself too weak to go to visit Ganymede, and therefore he desired his brother to go and tell Ganymede, "whom," said Orlando, "I in sport do call my Rosalind," the accident which had befallen him.

---

49 remorse [rɪˈmɔːrs] (n.) 痛悔；自責
50 repent [rɪˈpent] (v.) 悔悟；悔改
51 penitent [ˈpenɪtənt] (a.) 悔過的；懺悔的

🎧63 Thither then Oliver went, and told to Ganymede and Aliena how Orlando had saved his life; and when he had finished the story of Orlando's bravery and his own providential[52] escape he owned to them that he was Orlando's brother who had so cruelly used him; and then be told them of their reconciliation[53].

The sincere sorrow that Oliver expressed for his offenses made such a lively impression on the kind heart of Aliena that she instantly fell in love with him; and Oliver observing how much she pitied the distress he told her he felt for his fault, he as suddenly fell in love with her.

But while love was thus stealing into the hearts of Aliena and Oliver, he was no less busy with Ganymede, who, hearing of the danger Orlando had been in, and that he was wounded by the lioness, fainted; and when he recovered he pretended that he had counterfeited[54] the swoon[55] in the imaginary character of Rosalind, and Ganymede said to Oliver: "Tell your brother Orlando how well I counterfeited a swoon."

---

52 providential [ˌprɑːvɪˈdenʃəl] (a.) 天佑的
53 reconciliation [ˌrekənsɪliˈeɪʃən] (n.) 和解
54 counterfeit [ˈkaʊntərfɪt] (v.) 偽造
55 swoon [swuːn] (n.) 昏厥

🎧 **64** But Oliver saw by the paleness of his complexion that he did really faint, and, much wondering at the weakness of the young man, he said, "Well, if you did counterfeit, take a good heart and counterfeit to be a man."

"So I do," replied Ganymede, truly, "but I should have been a woman by right."

Oliver made this visit a very long one, and when at last he returned back to his brother he had much news to tell him; for, besides the account of Ganymede's fainting at the hearing that Orlando was wounded, Oliver told him how he had fallen in love with the fair shepherdess Aliena, and that she had lent a favorable ear to his suit, even in this their first interview; and he talked to his brother, as of a thing almost settled, that he should marry Aliena, saying that he so well loved her that he would live here as a shepherd and settle his estate[56] and house at home upon Orlando.

"You have my consent," said Orlando. "Let your wedding be tomorrow, and I will invite the duke and his friends. Go and persuade your shepherdess to agree to this. She is now alone, for, look, here comes her brother."

---

56 estate [ɪˈsteɪt] (n.) 財產

🎧 65 Oliver went to Aliena, and Ganymede, whom Orlando had perceived approaching, came to inquire after the health of his wounded friend.

When Orlando and Ganymede began to talk over the sudden love which had taken place between Oliver and. Aliena, Orlando said be had advised his brother to persuade his fair shepherdess to be married on the morrow[57], and then he added how much he could wish to be married on the same day to his Rosalind.

Ganymede, who well approved of this arrangement, said that if Orlando really loved Rosalind as well as he professed to do, he should have his wish; for on the morrow he would engage to make Rosalind appear in her own person, and also that Rosalind should be willing to marry Orlando.

This seemingly wonderful event, which, as Ganymede was the Lady Rosalind, he could so easily perform, be pretended he would bring to pass by the aid of magic, which he said he had learned of an uncle who was a famous magician.

57 morrow [ˈmɔːrou] (n.) 翌日;次日

🎧66 The fond lover Orlando, half believing and half doubting what he heard, asked Ganymede if he spoke in sober[58] meaning.

"By my life I do," said Ganymede; "therefore put on your best clothes, and bid the duke and your friends to your wedding, for if you desire to be married tomorrow to Rosalind, she shall be here."

The next morning, Oliver having obtained the consent of Aliena, they came into the presence of the duke, and with them also came Orlando.

They being all assembled to celebrate this double marriage, and as yet only one of the brides appearing, there was much of wondering and conjecture, but they mostly thought that Ganymede was making a jest of Orlando.

The duke, hearing that it was his own daughter that was to be brought in this strange way, asked Orlando if he believed the shepherd-boy could really do what he had promised; and while Orlando was answering that he knew not what to think, Ganymede entered and asked the duke, if he brought his daughter, whether he would consent to her marriage with Orlando.

---

58 sober ['soubər] (a.) 認真的；嚴肅的

"That I would," said the duke, "if I had kingdoms to give with her."

Ganymede then said to Orlando, "And you say you will marry her if I bring her here."

"That I would," said Orlando, "if I were king of many kingdoms."

🎧 68 Ganymede and Aliena then went out together, and, Ganymede throwing off his male attire[59], and being once more dressed in woman's apparel, quickly became Rosalind without the power of magic; and Aliena, changing her country garb[60] for her own rich clothes, was with as little trouble transformed into the lady Celia.

While they were gone, the duke said to Orlando that he thought the shepherd Ganymede very like his daughter Rosalind; and Orlando said he also had observed the resemblance.

They had no time to wonder how all this would end, for Rosalind and Celia, in their own clothes, entered, and, no longer pretending that it was by the power of magic that she came there, Rosalind threw herself on her knees before her father and begged his blessing.

It seemed so wonderful to all present that she should so suddenly appear, that it might well have passed for magic; but Rosalind would no longer trifle with her father, and told him the story of her banishment, and of her dwelling in the forest as a shepherd-boy, her cousin Celia passing as her sister.

---

59 attire [ə'taɪr] (n.) 服裝
60 garb [gɑːrb] (n.)（某種職業或民族特有的）服裝；裝束

The duke ratified[61] the consent he had already given to the marriage; and Orlando and Rosalind, Oliver and Celia, were married at the same time. And though their wedding could not be celebrated in this wild forest with any of the parade of splendor usual on such occasions, yet a happier wedding-day was never passed.

And while they were eating their venison under the cool shade of the pleasant trees, as if nothing should be wanting to complete the felicity[62] of this good duke and the true lovers, an unexpected messenger arrived to tell the duke the joyful news that his dukedom was restored to him.

61 ratify ['rætɪfaɪ] (v.) 批准
62 felicity [fɪ'lɪsɪti] (n.) 〔文學用法〕幸福

70 The usurper, enraged at the flight of his daughter Celia, and hearing that every day men of great worth resorted to the forest of Arden to join the lawful duke in his exile, much envying that his brother should be so highly respected in his adversity, put himself at the head of a large force and advanced toward the forest, intending to seize his brother and put him with all his faithful followers to the sword; but by a wonderful interposition of Providence this bad brother was converted from his evil intention, for just as he entered the skirts of the wild forest he was met by an old religious man, a hermit, with whom he had much talk and who in the end completely turned his heart from his wicked design.

Thenceforward he became a true penitent, and resolved, relinquishing his unjust dominion, to spend the remainder of his days in a religious house. The first act of his newly conceived penitence was to send a messenger to his brother (as has been related) to offer to restore to him his dukedom, which be had usurped so long, and with it the lands and revenues of his friends, the faithful followers of his adversity.

🎧 **71** This joyful news, as unexpected as it was welcome, came opportunely to heighten the festivity and rejoicings at the wedding of the princesses. Celia complimented her cousin on this good, fortune which had happened to the duke, Rosalind's father, and wished her joy very sincerely, though she herself was no longer heir to the dukedom, but by this restoration which her father had made, Rosalind was now the heir, so completely was the love of these two cousins unmixed with anything of jealousy or of envy.

The duke had now an opportunity of rewarding those true friends who had stayed with him in his banishment; and these worthy followers, though they had patiently shared his adverse fortune, were very well pleased to return in peace and prosperity, to the palace of their lawful duke.

Celia

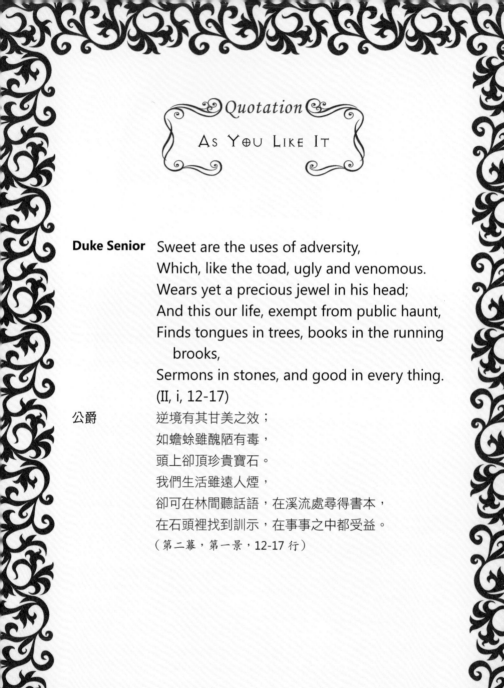

Quotation
As You Like It

Duke Senior Sweet are the uses of adversity,
Which, like the toad, ugly and venomous.
Wears yet a precious jewel in his head;
And this our life, exempt from public haunt,
Finds tongues in trees, books in the running
    brooks,
Sermons in stones, and good in every thing.
(II, i, 12-17)

公爵   逆境有其甘美之效;
如蟾蜍雖醜陋有毒,
頭上卻頂珍貴寶石。
我們生活雖遠人煙,
卻可在林間聽話語,在溪流處尋得書本,
在石頭裡找到訓示,在事事之中都受益。
(第二幕,第一景,12-17 行)

Jaques   All the world's a stage,
And all the men and women merely players;
They have their exits and their entrances,
And one man in his time plays many parts,
His acts being seven ages. (II, vii, 139-43)

杰奎思　整個世界即舞台，
一切男女皆演員；
都有退場有出場，
一生扮演多角色，
演出可分七階段。
（第二幕，第七景，139-43 行）

國家圖書館出版品預行編目資料

悦讀莎士比亞故事 .3, 仲夏夜之夢 & 皆大歡喜 / Charles
and Mary Lamb 著 ; Cosmos Language Workshop 譯 .
一初版 . 一 [臺北市] : 寂天文化，2011.11
　　面 ; 公分 .

ISBN 978-986-184-941-6 （25K 平裝附光碟片)

1. 英語　2. 讀本

805.18　　　　　　　　　　　　　　　　　10001

作者	Charles and Mary Lamb
譯者	Cosmos Language Workshop
主編	黃鈺云
內文排版	謝青秀
製程管理	林欣穎
出版者	寂天文化事業股份有限公司
電話	02-2365-9739
傳真	02-2365-9835
網址	www.icosmos.com.tw
讀者服務	onlineservice@icosmos.com.tw
出版日期	2011 年 11 月 初版一刷（250101）
	版權所有 請勿翻印
郵撥帳號	1998620-0 寂天文化事業股份有限公司
	訂購金額 600（含）元以上郵資免費
	訂購金額 600 元以下者，請外加郵資 60 元
	〔若有破損，請寄回更換，謝謝。〕